For the magical New Zealand teller, Liz Miller,
who told me this delightful story

—M.R.M.

For Nicholas and John

—M.N.D.

Manufactured in China.

Library of Congress Cataloging-in-Publication Data
MacDonald, Margaret Read.
The squeaky door / retold by Margaret Read MacDonald ; illustrated by Mary Newell DePalma.
p.   cm.— 1st ed.
   Summary: When Little Boy is frightened by a squeaky bedroom door, his grandmother brings
in various animals to help him feel secure enough to sleep. Includes notes on the story's origins.
   ISBN-10: 0-06-028373-4 — ISBN-10: 0-06-028374-2 (lib. bdg.)
   ISBN-13: 978-0-06-028373-5 — ISBN-13: 978-0-06-028374-2 (lib. bdg.)
   [1. Folklore—Puerto Rico. 2. Bedtime—Folklore. 3. Grandmothers—Folklore. 4. Domestic animals—
Fiction.] I. Title. II. DePalma, Mary Newell, ill.
PZ8.1+   2004030641   398.2 [E] 22   CIP   AC

Typography by Amelia May Anderson
1 2 3 4 5 6 7 8 9 10 ❖ First Edition

The squeaky Door

retold by
Margaret Read MacDonald

pictures by
Mary Newell DePalma

HarperCollinsPublishers

Little Boy went to Grandma's house to spend the night.
Grandma said,
"I have a surprise for you!
You get to sleep in the big brass bed all by yourself!
But... are you going to be scared?"

Little Boy said, "NO. Not ME!"

Grandma tucked the boy in.
She kissed the boy good night... SMACK!

"Now, when I go out and turn
off the light and close the door...
are you going to be scared?"

"NO. Not ME!"

So Grandma tip...toed...out.
She turned...off...the light...Click.
She closed...the...door...s q u e e e e a k...

Little Boy began to cry.

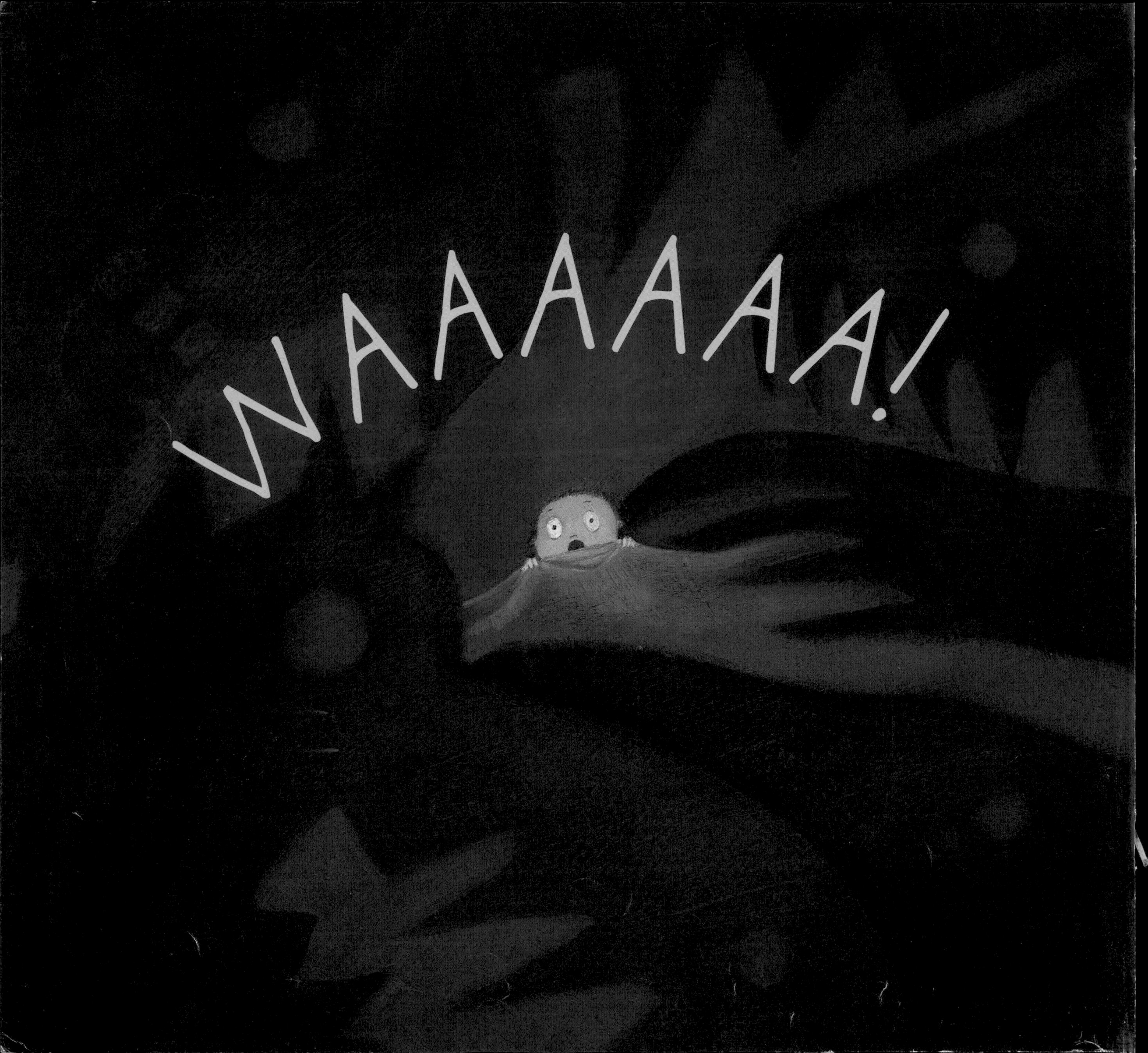
WAAAAAA!

Grandma ran back inside.

"Oh my goodness! Were you scared?"

"NO. Not ME!"

"I think you were scared.
How would you like to sleep with the cat?"

"YES! YES! YES!"

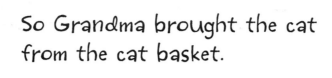

So Grandma brought the cat
from the cat basket.

She tucked the cat in.

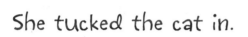

She kissed the cat good night. SMACK!
She kissed the boy good night. SMACK!

"Now, when I go out and turn off
the light and close the door...
are you going to be scared?"

"NO. Not ME!"

So Grandma tip...toed...out.
She turned...off...the light...Click.
She closed...the...door...

squeeeeeak!

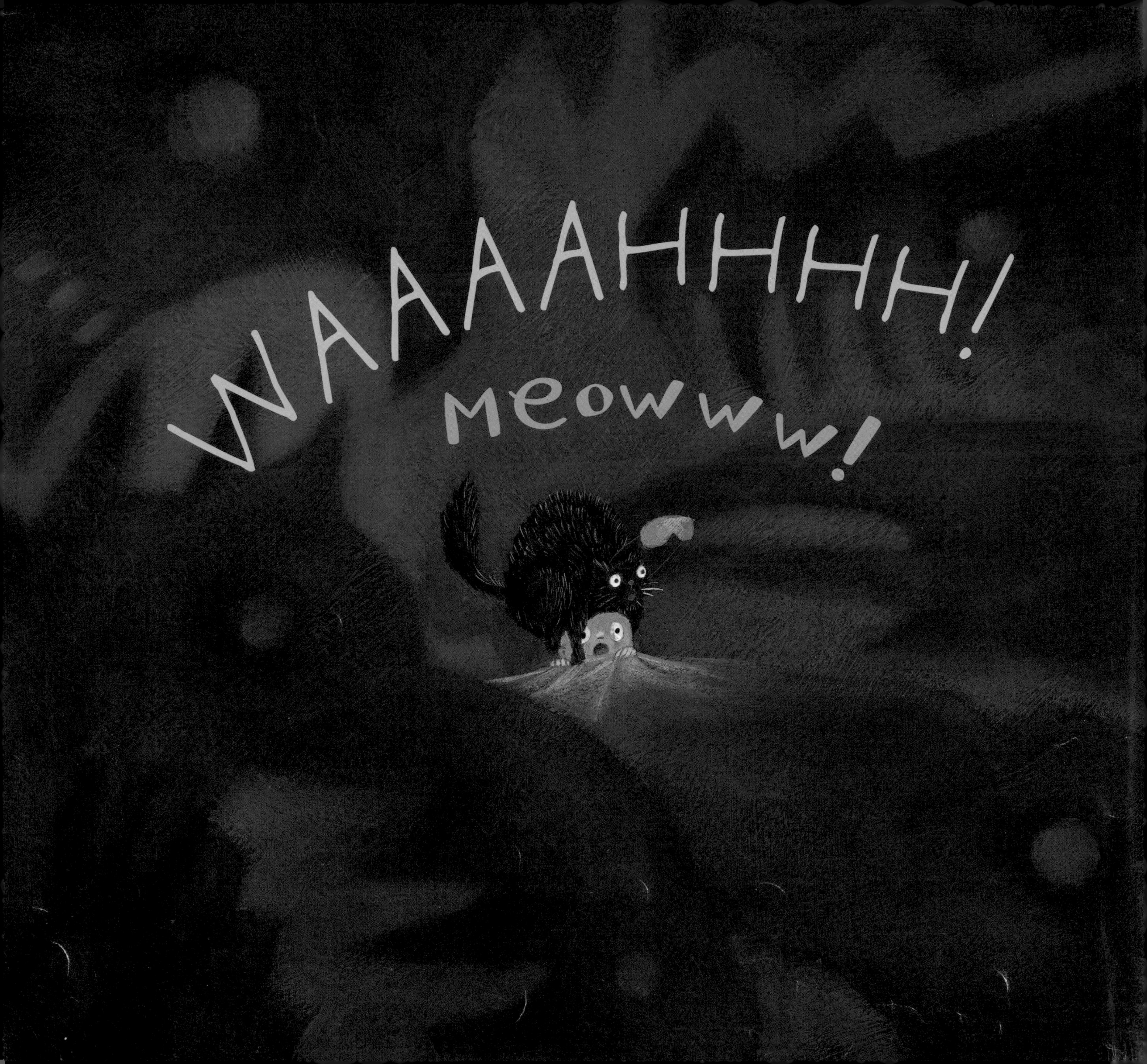
WAAAAAHHHHH!
meowww!

"Oh my goodness! Were you scared?"

"NO. Not ME!"

"How would you like to sleep with the dog?"

"YES! YES! YES!"

So Grandma brought the dog
from the doghouse.

She tucked the dog in.

She kissed the boy good night. SMACK!
She kissed the cat good night. SMACK!
She kissed the dog good night. SMACK!

"Now, when I go out and turn off the light and close the door... are you going to be scared?"

"NO. Not ME!"

So Grandma tip...toed...out.
She turned...off...the light... Click.
She closed...the...door...

eeeak.

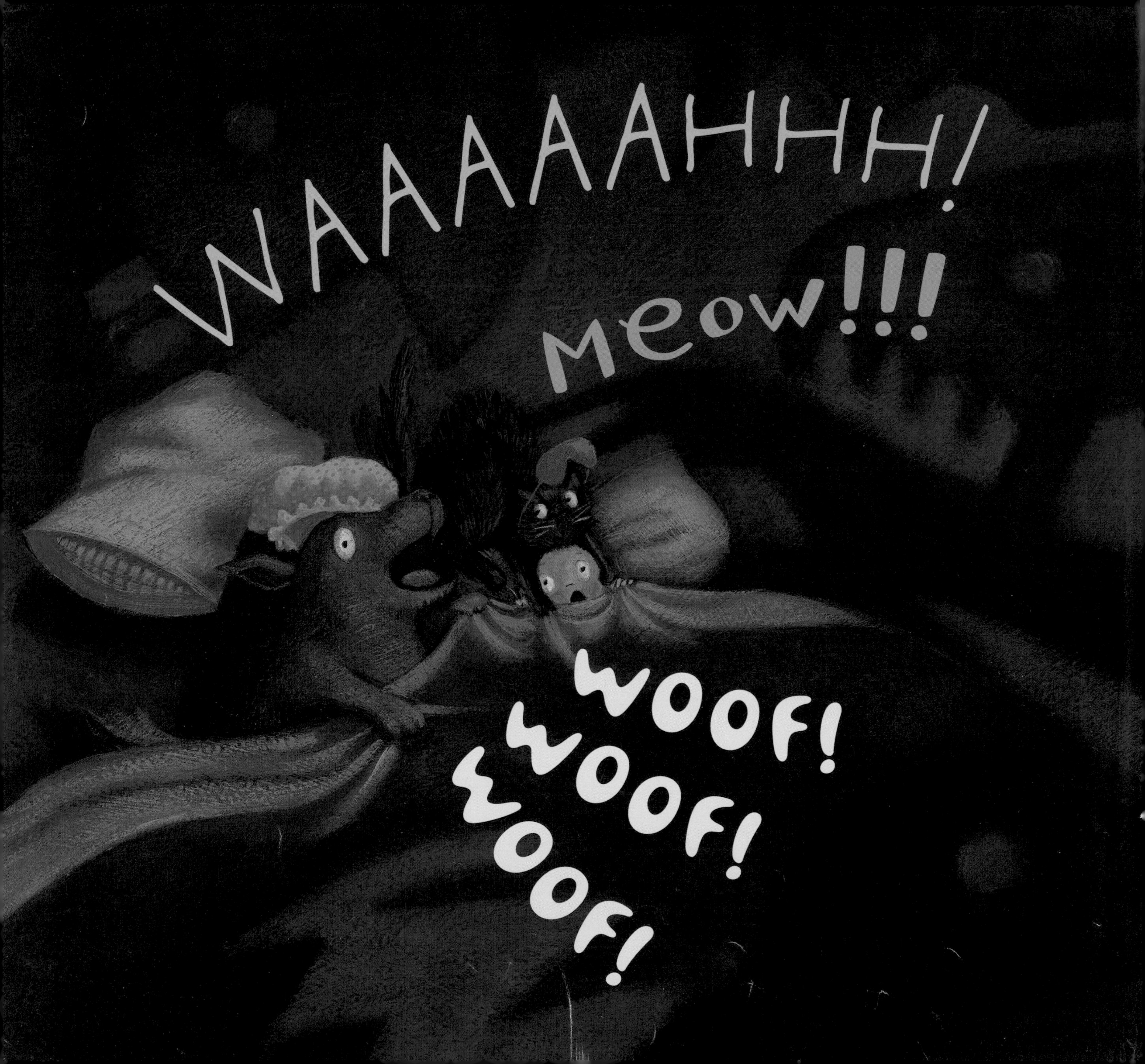
WAAAAAAHHH!
meow!!!
WOOF!
WOOF!
WOOF!

"Oh my goodness. Were you scared?"

"NO. Not ME!"

"I know! Would you like to sleep with the pig?"

"YES! YES! YES!"

So Grandma brought the pig
from the pigpen.

She tucked the pig in.

She kissed the boy good night. SMACK!
She kissed the cat good night. SMACK!
She kissed the dog good night. SMACK!
She kissed the PIG good night (yuck). SMACK!

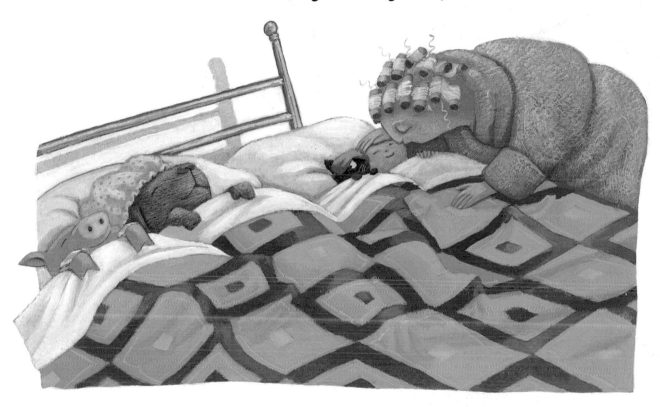

"Now, when I go out and turn off
the light and close the door...
are you going to be scared?"

"NO. Not ME!"

So Grandma tip...toed...out.
She turned...off...the light...Click.
She closed...the...door...

squeeeak!

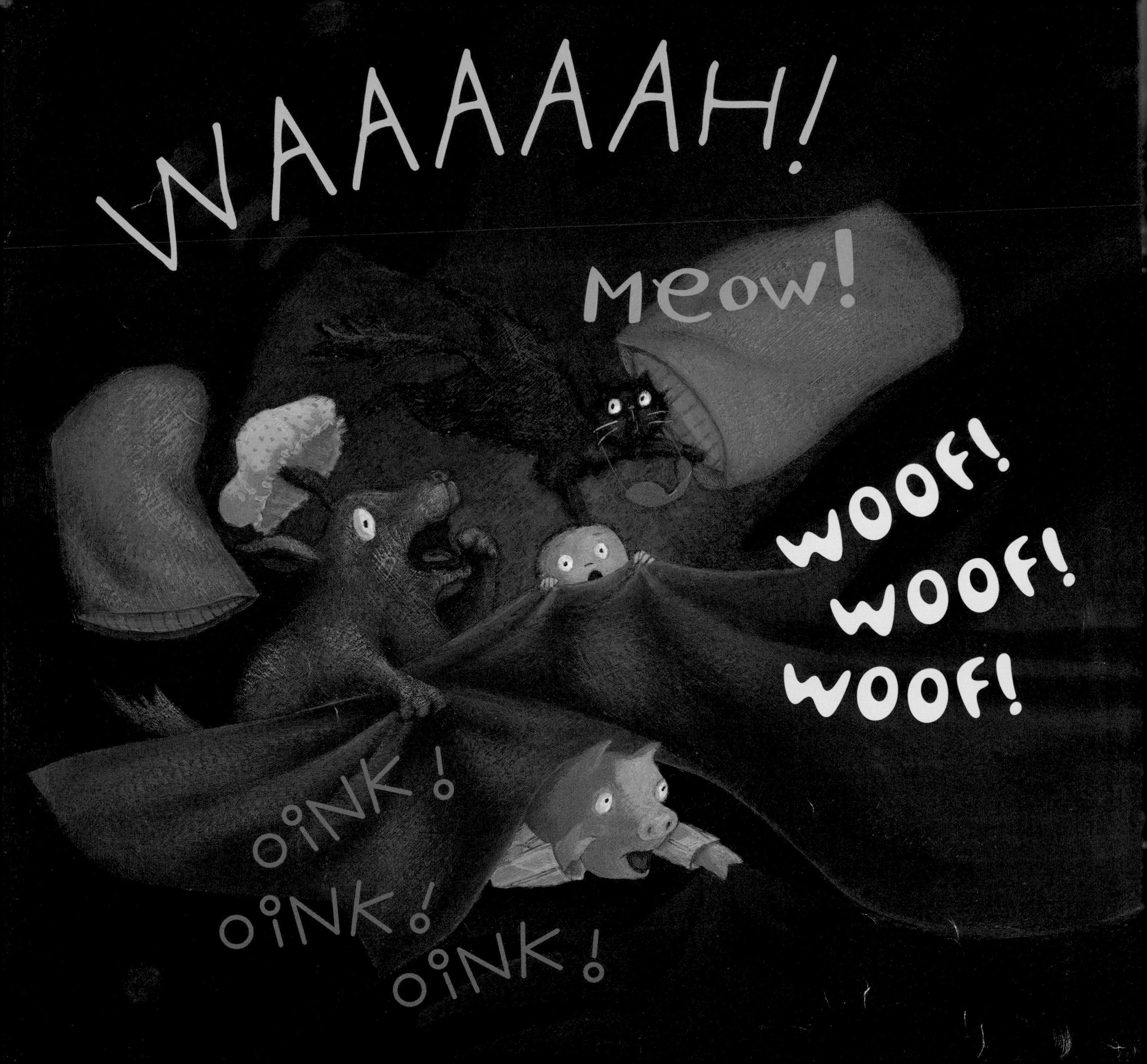
WAAAAAH!
meow!
WOOF!
WOOF!
WOOF!
OINK!
OINK!
OINK!

"Oh my goodness! Were you scared?"

"NO. Not ME!"

"I have an idea! Why don't you sleep with . . . the HORSE!"

"YES! YES! YES!"

So Grandma went out to the stable and got the horse.

She tucked the horse in.

Then...
She kissed the boy good night. SMACK!
She kissed the cat good night. SMACK!
She kissed the dog good night. SMACK!
She kissed the pig good night (yuck). SMACK!
She kissed the horse good night. SMACK!

"Now, when I go out and turn off the
light and close the door...
are you going to be scared?"

"NO. Not ME!"

So Grandma tip...toed...out.
She turned...off...the light...Click.
She closed...the...door...

squeeeak!

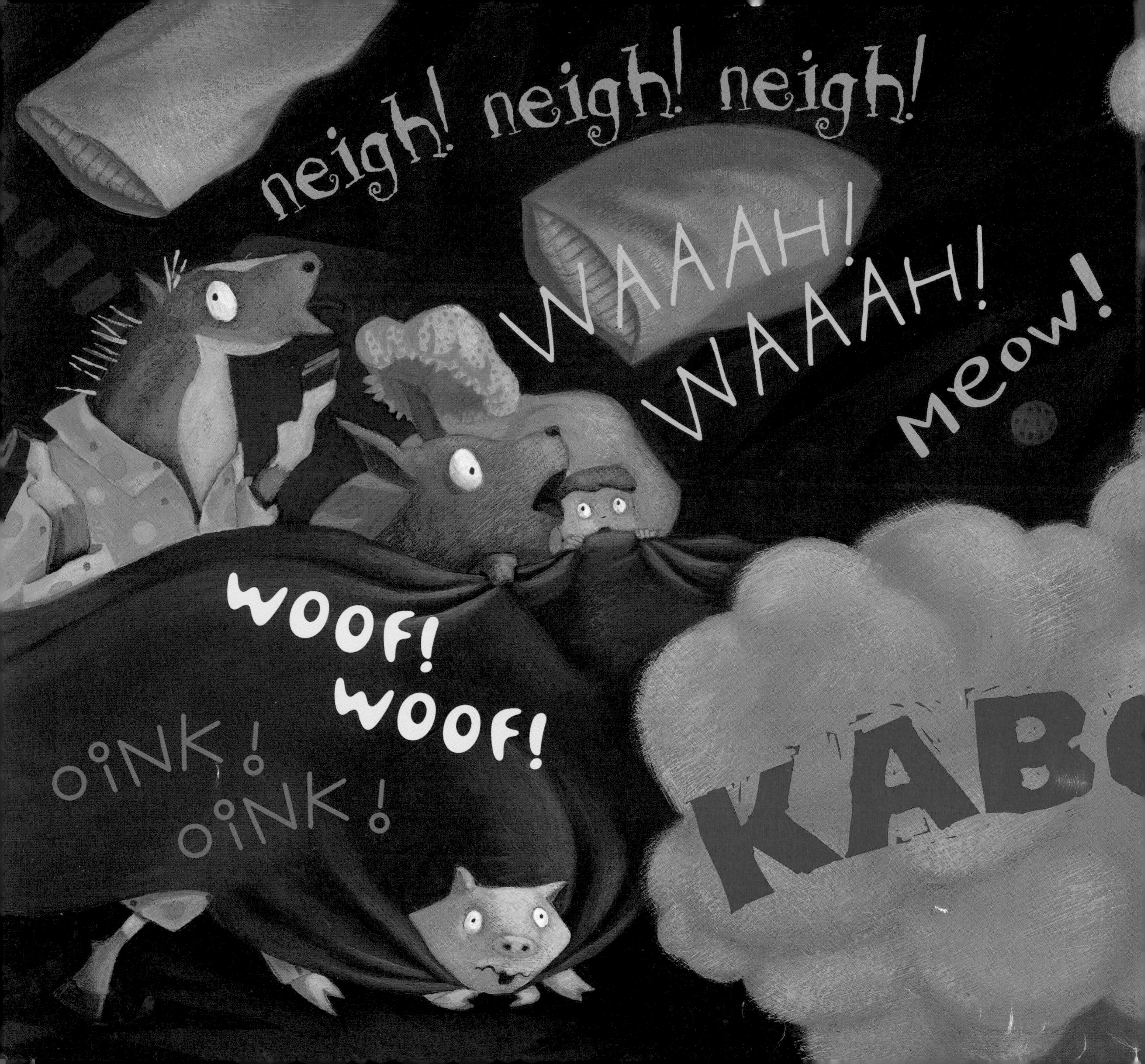
neigh! neigh! neigh!
WAAAH!
WAAAH!
meow!
WOOF!
WOOF!
OINK!
OINK!
KAB

The bed broke.

"Oh my goodness.
This will never do.
This will never do."

Grandma put the horse back.

She put the pig back.

She put the dog back.

She put the cat back.

Grandma put Little Boy in bed
with her and Grandpa that night.

And next morning...

Grandma got out her tool chest.
She FIXED that broken bed.

Then she got out her oilcan.
She OILED that squeaky door.

squeeeak...squeeeak...
gLub...gLub...gLub...gLub...
squeeeak...squeeeak...
gLub...gLub...gLub...gLub...
squeeeak...squeeeak...
gLub...gLub...gLub...

No sound at all..."YES!"

And that night Grandma
tucked Little Boy in.
She tucked the cat in.
And nobody else.

Then...
She kissed the boy good night. SMACK!
She kissed the cat good night. SMACK!

"Now, when I go out and turn off
the light and close the door...
are you going to be scared?"

"NO. Not ME!"

So Grandma tip...toed...out.
She turned...off...the light...Click.
She closed...the...door...sssshhhh...

She listened.
She heard Little Boy snoring.
She heard the cat snoring.

AhnhMMMM...AhnhMMMM
AhnhMMMMM...AhnhMMMMM

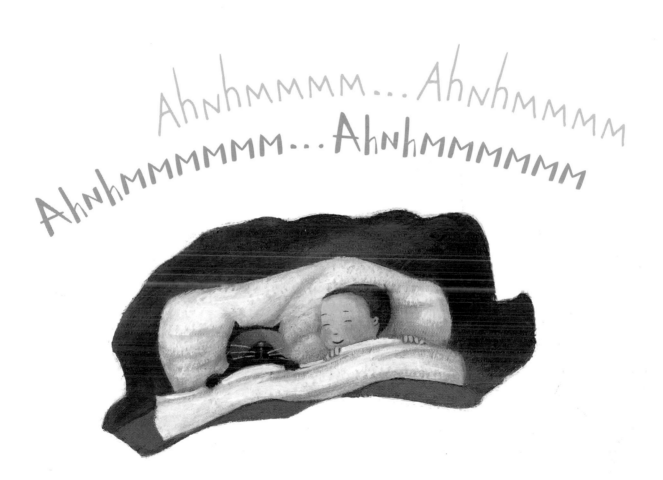

And that's the story of Grandma, Little Boy, and the squeaky door.

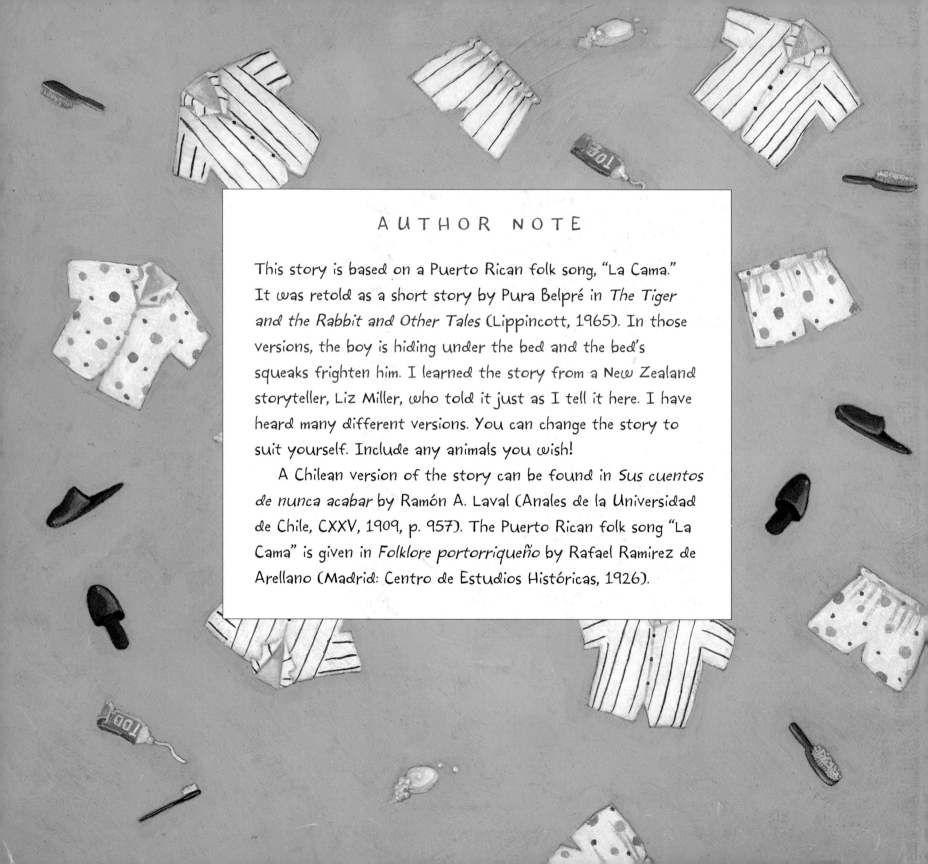

AUTHOR NOTE

This story is based on a Puerto Rican folk song, "La Cama."
It was retold as a short story by Pura Belpré in *The Tiger
and the Rabbit and Other Tales* (Lippincott, 1965). In those
versions, the boy is hiding under the bed and the bed's
squeaks frighten him. I learned the story from a New Zealand
storyteller, Liz Miller, who told it just as I tell it here. I have
heard many different versions. You can change the story to
suit yourself. Include any animals you wish!

A Chilean version of the story can be found in *Sus cuentos
de nunca acabar* by Ramón A. Laval (Anales de la Universidad
de Chile, CXXV, 1909, p. 957). The Puerto Rican folk song "La
Cama" is given in *Folklore portorriqueño* by Rafael Ramirez de
Arellano (Madrid: Centro de Estudios Históricas, 1926).